Katie Woo

Make-Believe Class

by Fran Manushkin

illustrated by Tammie Lyon

PICTURE WINDOW BOOKS

a capstone imprint

Katie Woo is published by Picture Window Books,
A Capstone Imprint
151 Good Counsel Drive, P.O. Box 669
Mankato, Minnesota, MN 56002
www.capstonepub.com

Text © 2010 Fran Manushkin
Illustrations © 2010 Picture Window Books

Printed in the United States of America in Melrose Park, Illinois.
092009
005620LKS10

Library of Congress Cataloging-in-Publication Data
Manushkin, Fran.
    Make-believe class / by Fran Manushkin; illustrated by Tammie Lyon.
    p. cm. — (Katie Woo)
    ISBN 978-1-4048-5732-2 (library binding)
    [1. Imagination—Fiction. 2. Schools—Fiction.] I. Lyon, Tammie, ill. II. Title.
PZ7.M3195Mak 2010   2009030617
[E]—dc22

Summary: One cold, gray, winter day, Miss Winkle leads Katie Woo and the rest of her
class on an imaginary journey, challenging them to find ways to complete their lessons
on a sunny island, under the sea, or on the moon.

Art Director: Kay Fraser
Graphic Designer: Emily Harris
Production Specialist: Michelle Biedscheid

Photo Credits
Fran Manushkin, pg. 26
Tammie Lyon, pg. 26

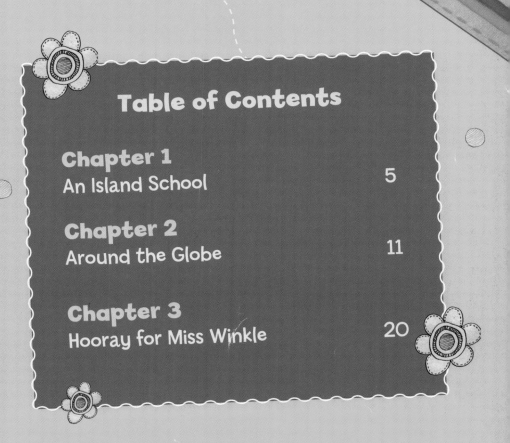

Table of Contents

Chapter 1
An Island School

It was a cold gray day.

Miss Winkle told her

class, "Let's make up a story

together. It will help us

forget this winter day."

Katie raised her hand.

"I have an idea!" she said.

"Let's pretend our school is

in a warm, sunny place."

Miss Winkle smiled. "Let's put our school on an island," she said.

"Great!" said Pedro. "We will get there on a sailboat instead of a bus!"

"But how will we do our math?" asked Miss Winkle.

"I know!" JoJo said. "We will add up the seagulls when they land."

"And subtract them when they fly away," said Katie.

"We can't write on paper," said Miss Winkle. "The wind will blow it away."

"I know!" said JoJo. "We can write in the wet sand."

"We won't need erasers,"
said Katie. "The sea will take
away our mistakes."

Chapter 2
Around the Globe

"I want to go to school

in Australia," shouted Peter.

"It's upside down there!"

"That is only on the globe," said Miss Winkle. "It's not really upside down."

"Good!" said Susie. "I would get so dizzy!"

"Let's go to school on the moon!" yelled Chuck. "It would be so cool!"

"We can draw pictures of the Earth floating in space," said JoJo. "It's a good science lesson!"

"And a great art lesson too!" said Miss Winkle.

"Gym class would be the best!" said Katie. "On the earth, I can't jump high. But on the moon, I could fly!"

"But the moon is so gray," said Pedro. "I would miss the nice green earth."

"Let's ride our rocket back,

and land in the sea!" said

Miss Winkle. "We will study

the fish underwater."

"Sea turtles are neat too!"

shouted Chuck.

"Sharks are not," warned Susie. "Let's sail back to land."

"I agree," said JoJo. "I want to see Washington, D.C."

"We can have our class at the U.S. Mint!" said Miss Winkle. "That's where they make all our money!"

Katie joked, "Math class would last forever! There is so much money to count!"

Chapter 3

Hooray for Miss Winkle

"Look!" Miss Winkle pointed out the window. "It's snowing! The first snow of the year!"

"I want to stay here!" said Katie. "There is no snow on a warm island."

"Or on the moon!" yelled JoJo.

"And you can't make snowballs in the sea," added Pedro. "Or at the U.S. Mint."

"I think it snows in
Australia," said Miss Winkle.
"But I am not sure."

"I am sure about one thing," said Katie. "Miss Winkle is a terrific teacher! She turned a gray day into a happy one!"

"Hooray for Miss Winkle!" everyone shouted.

Then the recess bell rang, and they all went out to play!

About the Author

Fran Manushkin is the author of many popular picture books, including *How Mama Brought the Spring; Baby, Come Out!; Latkes and Applesauce: A Hanukkah Story;* and *The Tushy Book.* There is a real Katie Woo — she's Fran's great-niece — but she never gets in half the trouble of the Katie Woo in the books. Fran writes on her beloved Mac computer in New York City, without the help of her two naughty cats, Cookie and Goldy.

About the Illustrator

Tammie Lyon began her love for drawing at a young age while sitting at the kitchen table with her dad. She continued her love of art and eventually attended the Columbus College of Art and Design, where she earned a bachelors degree in fine art. After a brief career as a professional ballet dancer, she decided to devote herself full time to illustration. Today she lives with her husband, Lee, in Cincinnati, Ohio. Her dogs, Gus and Dudley, keep her company as she works in her studio.

Glossary

Australia (ah-STRAYL-yuh)—a continent southeast of Asia; it is the smallest continent

eraser (ee-RAY-sur)—something used to rub off pencil or pen marks

island (EYE-luhnd)—a piece of land surrounded by water

science (SIGH-uhnss)—the study of nature and the physical world by testing, experimenting, and measuring

seagulls (SEE-guhlz)—gray and white birds found near the sea

terrific (tuh-RIF-ick)—very good

underwater (UHN-dur-WAW-tur)—located, used, or done under the surface of water

Discussion Questions

1. Miss Winkle's class used their imaginations to make their gray day more fun. What do you do to have fun on cold gray days?

2. What do you think would be served for lunch at a school on a hot and sunny island?

3. The class thought it would be fun to have science and gym on the moon. What class do you think would be more fun on the moon than on Earth?

Writing Prompts

1. Peter wants to go to school in Australia. Research Australia, and write a paragraph about the country.

2. The students talk about going to school underwater. Imagine what kind of playground they would have underwater. Draw it, and write a sentence to describe it.

3. Have you ever taken a class trip? Write a paragraph about it.

Having Fun
with Katie Woo

In *Make-Believe Class*, Katie and her classmates take a trip all over the universe. Think about a trip you've taken. It could be the trip to your grandparents', the ride to school, or the walk to the grocery store.

Now make a map of your trip. Here's how you do it!

What you need:

- large piece of paper
- a pencil
- a ruler
- markers or crayons

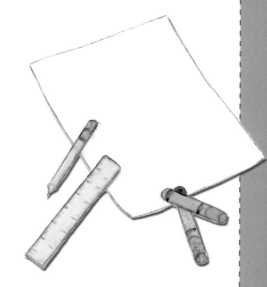

What you do:

1. What special places or landmarks do you see on your trip? Put them on the map. Think of buildings, trees, hills, parks, and other things that stand out along the way.

2. Draw your starting point on one side of the page. Then draw the path. Remember to add turns where you need them. Finally, draw your end spot.

3. Now add your landmarks from step one. Use lots of colors to make the landmarks stand out.

4. Add a key to your map. A key is a list or chart that explains symbols, like the landmarks, used on your map.